<u>Nev</u>er Babysit the Hippopotamuses!

Henry Holt and Company, Inc.
Publishers since 1866
115 West 18th Street
New York, New York 10011

Henry Holt is a registered trademark of Henry Holt and Company, Inc.

Published in Canada by Fitzhenry & Whiteside Ltd.,
195 Allstate Parkway, Markham, Ontario L3R 4T8.

Library of Congress Cataloging-in-Publication Data
Johnson, Doug.
Never babysit the hippopotamuses!/Doug Johnson; illustrated by Abby Carter.
Summary: Babysitting hippopotamuses leads to wacky events and unruly incidents.
[1. Hippopotamus—Fiction. 2. Babysitters—Fiction.] I. Carter, Abby, ill. II. Title.
PZ7.J631715Ne 1993 [E]—dc20 93-18341

ISBN 0-8050-1873-5 (hardcover)
1 3 5 7 9 10 8 6 4 2
ISBN 0-8050-5029-9 (paperback)
1 3 5 7 9 10 8 6 4 2

First published in hardcover in 1993 by Henry Holt and Company, Inc.
First Owlet paperback edition, 1997

Printed in the United States of America on acid-free paper. ∞

Never Babysit the Hippopotamuses!

Doug Johnson illustrated by Abby Carter

Henry Holt and Company • New York

To Peggy, Christopher, Kyle, and Kelsey—
their love and laughter keep me young.
                            —D. J.

For Doug and Samantha
                —A. C.

Never babysit the Hippopotamuses.

To make them forget about their parents,
you'll have to play hide-and-seek....
You should pretend that they are very hard to find.

To let them get to know you, watch a TV show.
But don't watch a scary one, or they'll make you
look for monsters in the closet…under the beds…
in the basement…and even up the chimney.

And be careful if they ask you to dance.
The Hippopotamuses have very big feet.

Don't play leapfrog with them, they can be hard to jump over.

Don't play horsey either.
They always want you to be the horsey.

Oh, never babysit the Hippopotamuses!
They like to play cops and robbers, pirates…

...and lion tamer.

And they love to wrestle....

Sometimes they will even let you win.

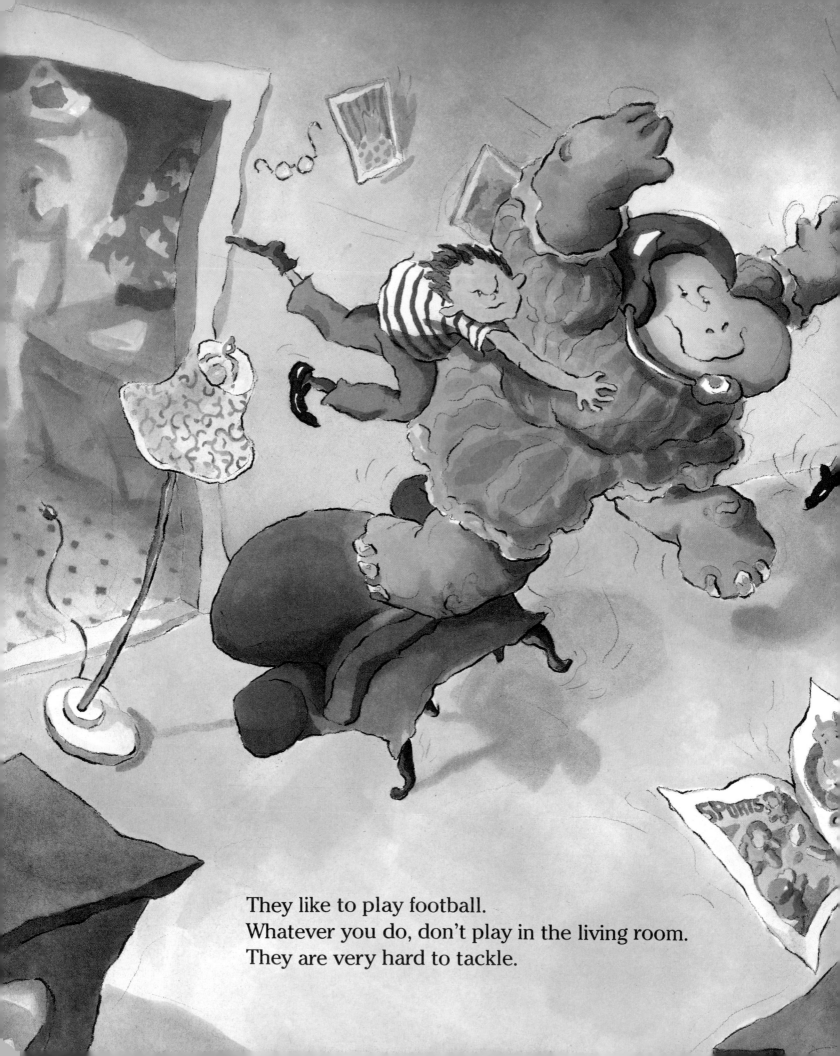

They like to play football.
Whatever you do, don't play in the living room.
They are very hard to tackle.

Before you get them ready for bed, you should
make them a snack. But don't make popcorn. They can eat a lot of it.

Oh, never, ever babysit the Hippopotamuses!
Bathtime is crazy.
The Hippos love to do cannonballs into the tub.

It can be quite difficult getting them into their pajamas.

Not to mention their slippers.

And brushing their teeth is not an easy job.

Oh, never, ever babysit the Hippopotamuses!

After you bring them to their room for bed,

they will surely start a pillow fight.

Then you will have to tuck them in and read them a bedtime story. Remember to turn on the night-light before you leave.

The Hippopotamuses are afraid of the dark,
and if you forget,
they will run out of their bedroom,

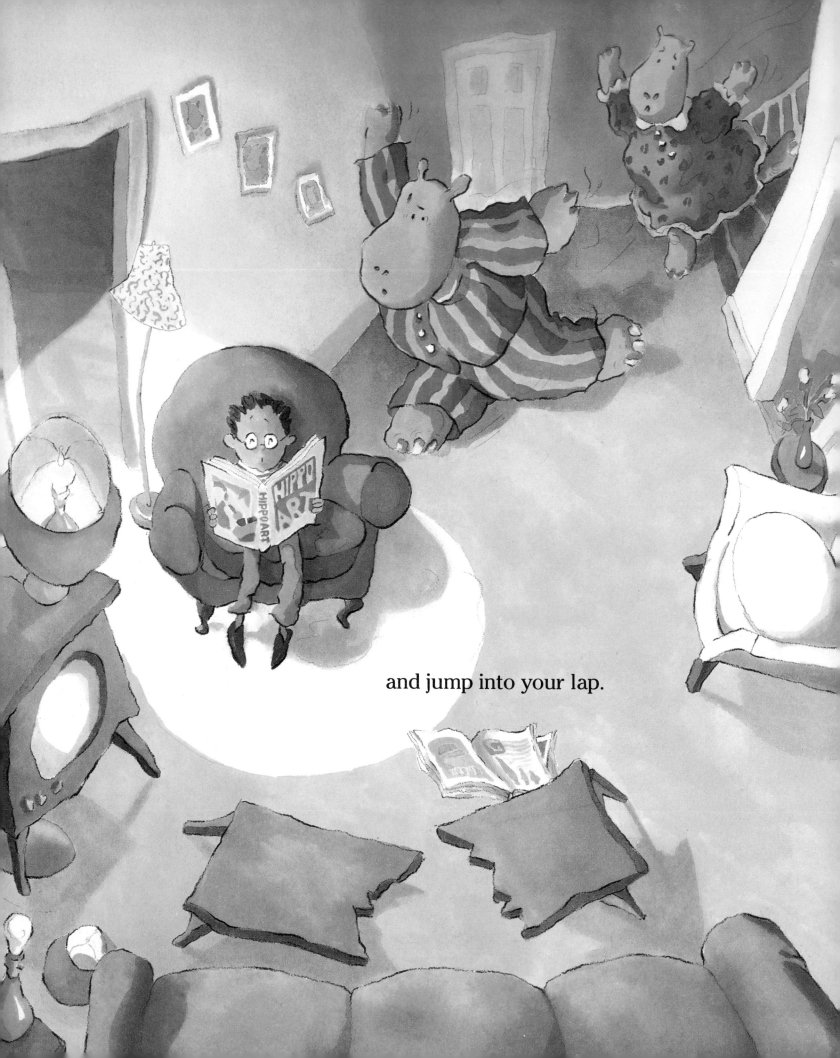

and jump into your lap.

By now it will be late, and their parents will be getting home soon.
You must be very firm. Stand on a ladder, look them in the eye, and holler:

"SIMMER DOWN AND GET INTO BED, HIPPOS! NOW!

So. Never babysit the Hippopotamuses.

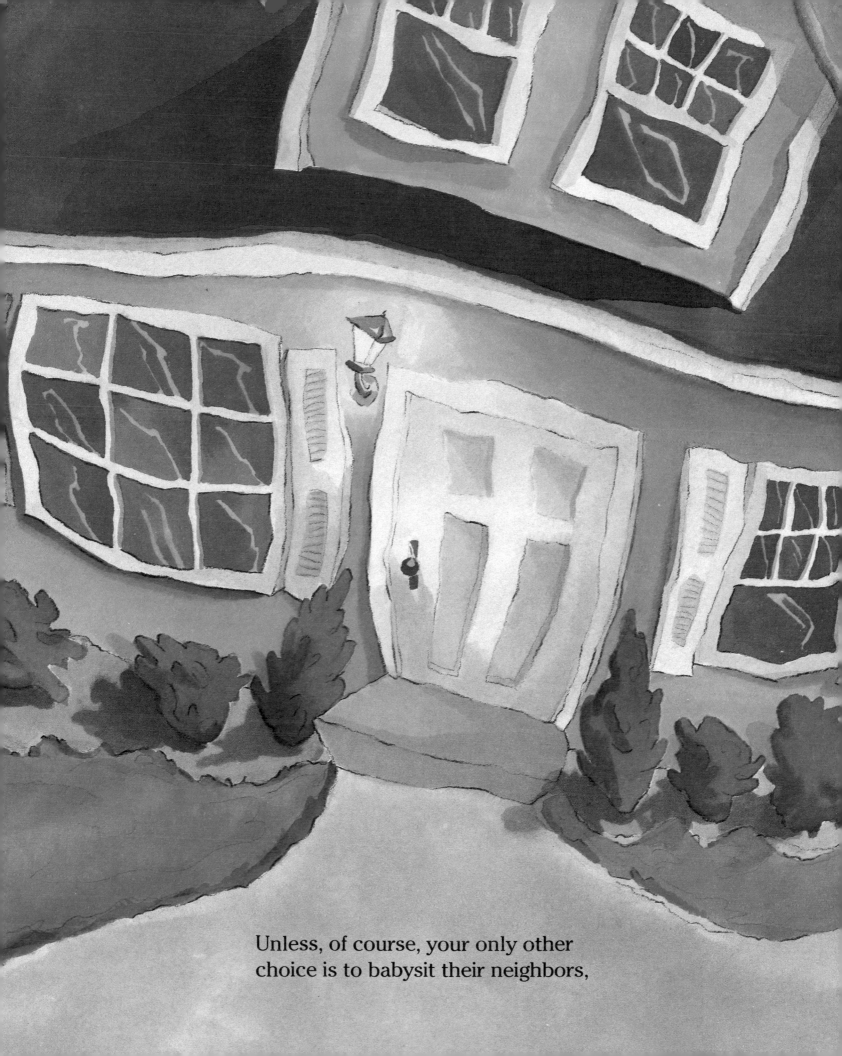

Unless, of course, your only other
choice is to babysit their neighbors,

the MONKEYS!